Hello, Brutus!

Aimee Aryal

Illustrated by M. De Angel & D. Moore

www.mascotbooks.com

It was a beautiful day at The Ohio State University. Brutus was on his way to Ohio Stadium for the big game.

At Mirror Lake he ran into OSU students. The students cheered, "Hello, Brutus!"

Brutus traveled to Orton Hall
where he ran into a professor.

The professor said, "Hello, Brutus!"

Brutus walked across the Oval and
passed by a group of alumni.

The alumni remembered Brutus
from their days at Ohio State.
They said, "Hello, again, Brutus!"

Brutus admired the statue of William Oxley Thompson, Ohio State's fifth president, in front of the Main Library.

A couple spotted Brutus and cheered,
"Hello, Brutus!"

Brutus continued on to University Hall,
one of the most historic buildings
on OSU's campus.

Brutus ran into a friend
outside University Hall.
The friend said, "Hello, Brutus!"

Brutus arrived at Ohio Stadium, home of the Buckeyes. He joined thousands of football fans for the big game.

Buckeye fans cheered, "Hello, Brutus!"

Brutus led the football team
onto the field.
He proudly waved an Ohio State flag.

The team cheered, "Hello, Brutus!"

The Buckeyes played
a great football game and
made all Ohio State fans proud.

After scoring a touchdown,
the quarterback yelled,
"Hello, Brutus!"

At halftime, The Ohio State Marching
Band performed "Across the Field".

They formed "Script Ohio" and a senior sousaphone player dotted the "i".

The Ohio State Buckeyes
won the football game!

The coach gave Brutus
a high-five and said,
"Buckeyes win, Brutus!"

After the game, Brutus was tired.
It had been a long day at
The Ohio State University.

He walked home and climbed into bed.
Good night, Brutus.

For Anna and Maya - Aimee Aryal

For more information about our products,
please visit us online at www.mascotbooks.com.

For more information, please contact Mascot Books,
P.O. Box 220157, Chantilly, VA 20153-0157

ISBN: 1-932888-51-9

Printed in the United States.

www.mascotbooks.com

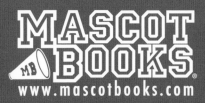

MLB

Boston Red Sox
Hello, Wally!
by Jerry Remy

New York Yankees
Let's Go, Yankees!
by Yogi Berra

New York Mets
Hello, Mr. Met!
by Rusty Staub

St. Louis Cardinals
Hello, Fredbird!
by Ozzie Smith

NFL

Dallas Cowboys
How 'Bout Them Cowboys!
by Aimee Aryal

NBA

Coming Soon

NHL

Coming Soon

Collegiate

Auburn University
War Eagle! by Pat Dye
Hello, Aubie! by Aimee Aryal

Boston College
Hello, Baldwin! by Aimee Aryal

Brigham Young University
Hello, Cosmo!
by Pat and LaVell Edwards

Clemson University
Hello, Tiger! by Aimee Aryal

Duke University
Hello, Blue Devil! by Aimee Aryal

Florida State University
Let's Go 'Noles! by Aimee Aryal

Georgia Tech
Hello, Buzz! by Aimee Aryal

Indiana University
Let's Go Hoosiers! by Aimee Aryal

James Madison University
Hello, Duke Dog! by Aimee Aryal

Louisiana State University
Hello, Mike! by Aimee Aryal

Michigan State University
Hello, Sparty! by Aimee Aryal

Mississippi State University
Hello, Bully! by Aimee Aryal

North Carolina State University
Hello, Mr. Wuf! by Aimee Aryal

Penn State University
Hello, Nittany Lion! by Aimee Aryal

Purdue University
Hello, Purdue Pete! by Aimee Aryal

Rutgers University
Hello, Scarlet Knight! by Aimee Aryal

Syracuse University
Hello, Otto! by Aimee Aryal

Texas A&M
Howdy, Reveille! by Aimee Aryal

UCLA
Hello, Joe Bruin! by Aimee Aryal

University of Alabama
Roll Tide! by Kenny Stabler
Hello, Big Al! by Aimee Aryal

University of Arkansas
Hello, Big Red! By Aimee Aryal

University of Connecticut
Hello, Jonathan! by Aimee Aryal

University of Florida
Hello, Albert! by Aimee Aryal

University of Georgia
How 'Bout Them Dawgs!
by Vince Dooley
Hello, Hairy Dawg! by Aimee Aryal

University of Illinois
Let's Go, Illini! by Aimee Aryal

University of Iowa
Hello, Herky! by Aimee Aryal

University of Kansas
Hello, Big Jay! by Aimee Aryal

University of Kentucky
Hello, Wildcat! by Aimee Aryal

University of Maryland
Hello, Testudo! by Aimee Aryal

University of Michigan
Let's Go, Blue! by Aimee Aryal

University of Minnesota
Hello, Goldy! by Aimee Aryal

University of Mississippi
Hello, Colonel Rebel! by Aimee Aryal

University of Nebraska
Hello, Herbie Husker! by Aimee Aryal

University of North Carolina
Hello, Rameses! by Aimee Aryal

University of Notre Dame
Let's Go Irish! by Aimee Aryal

University of Oklahoma
Let's Go Sooners! by Aimee Aryal

University of South Carolina
Hello, Cocky! by Aimee Aryal

University of Southern California
Hello, Tommy Trojan! by Aimee Aryal

University of Tennessee
Hello, Smokey! by Aimee Aryal

University of Texas
Hello, Hook 'Em! by Aimee Aryal

University of Virginia
Hello, CavMan! by Aimee Aryal

University of Wisconsin
Hello, Bucky! by Aimee Aryal

Virginia Tech
Yea, It's Hokie Game Day!
by Cheryl and Frank Beamer
Hello, Hokie Bird! by Aimee Aryal

Wake Forest University
Hello, Demon Deacon!
by Aimee Aryal

West Virginia University
Hello, Mountaineer! by Aimee Aryal

Road Races

Marine Corps Marathon
Run, Miles, Run! by Aimee Aryal

Crim Festival of Races
Running Bear and the Crim Kids!
by Su Nottingham

Visit us online at www.mascotbooks.com for a complete list of titles.